A WORLD OF *Storms*

ERIC S. ROBBINS

outskirts press

A World of Storms

v2.0

This is a work of fiction. The events and characters described herein are imaginary and are not intended to refer to specific places or living persons. The opinions expressed in this manuscript are solely the opinions of the author and do not represent the opinions or thoughts of the publisher. The author has represented and warranted full ownership and/or legal right to publish all the materials in this book.

Outskirts Press, Inc.
http://www.outskirtspress.com

ISBN: 978-1-9772-0877-4

PRINTED IN THE UNITED STATES OF AMERICA

ACKNOWLEDGMENTS

I was told as a child by many that I have a vivid imagination and a natural ability to write short stories. The recent passing of my mother gave me the desire to complete this novel. It was an obvious way for me to deal with the pain of her death. I've spent numerous of days thinking of writing my story, but didn't take the initiative to complete my work. A few days after my mother's death, she came to me in a dream and said "Eric, Finish it." This is my first novel and God gets all the praise! Once again, I would like to thank God and dedicate this novel to my late grandmother Mary Evelyn Gauntt and my late mother Patricia Ann Robbins. They were a great team and did a wonderful job on keeping me motivated in making good life choices. When I was younger, I thought about quitting school and my grandmother talked me out of it. She mentioned a short story to me, it was about a guy that was 23 years old that finished high school at that age. She stated that this guy didn't give up on school and now he's a doctor. That story motivated me to finish school while receiving multiple degrees and it shaped me into the person that I am today. I one day asked my grandmother about this guy and she started to laugh. It was that moment, that I realized that she made this story up. Thanks Mary Evelyn Gauntt, for you, I am thankful for each opportunity that's placed in front of me. I told myself one day, that I must do something that I've never done to get to where I would like to be in life. This is that opportunity and I plan to take full advantage!

CHAPTER 1

"Good morning, Mother. What's for breakfast this morning?"

"We have pancakes, sausages, and eggs, son." I was so excited! "You're the best cook ever! I would love for you to teach me how to make those great pancakes one day." She looked at me and smiled.

That was my beautiful mother, Mrs. Jenny, known around the town for her great spirit. She was always singing Christian songs while being in a good mood. My mom went to church every Sunday and she was very involved with most church activities. I think it's safe to say that she spent more time in church than at home. She was a beautiful black woman with brown eyes who stood at about 5 foot 8. Mom disliked when I'd take my time after hearing her call my name.

"Eric, please come and eat your breakfast before it gets cold," Mom said. I knew the consequences if I allowed my food to get cold. I moved in a hurry before she'd ask again.

Eric, well that would be me! I was a sixteen-year-old junior in high school. My mother did not play about food sitting on the table for long periods of time. She always taught me to be on time, it showed great character.

"Here I come, Mom, sorry for the wait." I could smell the food as I entered the dining area.

As I approached the table I saw my only sister

sitting there, shaking her head at me as I took a seat to eat my meal. Brooke took after our mother. Brooke had Mom's pretty brown eyes and she stood at about 5 foot 3 inches at the age of fifteen. She had a tomboyish thing going on and also happened to have great basketball skills. I was hoping that she would earn a basketball scholarship; that would make our family so proud. It was unfortunate that we attended such a small school, and it was almost impossible to get sport scholarships. Brooke played on the varsity team at Overlook High School in our small town outside of Greenville, South Carolina. We loved the area and the school regardless of the population.

Breakfast was great, and soon it was time to head out for the last week of school with my sister. As we approached the bench area that was designed for waiting on the school bus, the wind started to blow and I really enjoyed the cool breeze, although, it was uncommon for this time of the year. I was excited about summer break, which was coming up in a few days. As the bus approached, we stood firm as it pulled up in front of us and the stop sign flagged out for ongoing traffic to stop. As I walked to my seat, which was in the very back of the bus, I saw my best friend Ethen holding my spot. Ethen was very friendly and considerate. He liked to listen to other people's problems and he happened to be very understanding. He was pretty good at reading others within minutes of being around them. He had always told me that I was destined to do great things in life, but it always seemed to go in one ear and out the other. He was my best friend so I heard it all the time. As we were getting off the bus, I got this weird feeling, which came over me every time I saw the school building from this angle. This was a very small school, and it was built like a haunted church. This was a 2A school and teachers were able to give more attention to the students. It was only big enough to hold up to 200 people. As the bell rang, we hurried to get to class because the next bell would be the tardy bell. By the way, who wanted to deal with principal Mr. Fletcher? His attitude was horrible—so horrible that his assistant principal Mr. Daniels walked off the job and quit after having a problem within the office. Principal Fletcher had a strict demeanor and did not smile at any students, regardless of their accomplishments. All he cared about, was students getting to class on time and walking the halls with a hall pass.

I had to get to my next class, which was Mrs.

Smith's class. As I walk into Mrs. Annie Smith's class I had this feeling of fear and my mother always said that God did not create fear but it was hard for me to apply this concept in this math class. This was the only class that I have struggled with all year. Mrs. Smith was a nice teacher, however, this was not my subject. She was standing there with her long blonde hair and pretty blues eyes wearing a long blue dress, which complemented her eyes. There was no need for her to wear glasses because she liked wearing contacts instead. Here we go, she was putting the math questions on the board from last night's homework. My heart started pounding as I hoped that I did not get called to answer any of the questions in the lesson. I asked to go to the restroom to get out of getting called to the board. I left so quick that I forgot to ask for the hall pass. As

I was walking down the hall, I had my head down and I walked into someone. Who could this be? Even though I had my head down, I walked on my side of the hall. How could I bump into someone?

"Excuse me, sir, I didn't mean to bump into you." I smelled a musk smell before I had an opportunity to look up. It was only one person that I could think of that was allergic to deodorant.

When I looked up, I saw the last face that I wanted to see in the hallway without a hall pass. It was Principal Fletcher!

CHAPTER 2

"Mr. Fletcher, how are you doing today? That is a nice shirt that you are wearing." That was the first thing that came to mind.

"Do not flatter me, boy," said a grumpy old Mr. Fletcher. "Why are we not in class, Eric?"

All I could do was tell the truth.

"Mr. Fletcher, I actually left my hall pass in the classroom because I was in such a rush to go to the bathroom."

It was rare that he would cut student breaks.

He looked at me with disappointment and didn't smile.

"You need to hurry and get back to class, son," said Fletcher. "I'm going to cut you a break this time; however, please don't allow me to catch you in this hallway again."

"Yes Mr. Fletcher, I will not forget my pass next time."

Mr. Fletcher nodded his head at me and continued to scan the hallways for other students. As I was walking along the halls on my way back to class, I noticed that I'd been gone the majority of the class time. I sure hope Mrs. Smith did not count me absent, because she had done that in the past. I'd been working so hard on my grades this term; I would hate to mess up now. If I had a slip up, my mother would be disappointed because she knows that I'm more than capable of making an A in this class. The bell rang and class was over. There were students everywhere trying to get to their next class. It was my P.E. time next, and during this time we liked playing basketball. As we were picking teams, I saw my best friend Ethen walk in. He loved to play basketball as long as he could control the ball.

"Ethen, would you like to play ball on my team?"

"Sure," said Ethen, "as long as I can run point guard." Ethen was decent at the point position but he didn't play for Overlook High. After the scrimmage game, all the players took water breaks and discussed details of the previous games. As I looked at the time, it was almost time for the bell to rang.

"I'm ready to go home; this has been a long day," I said. The bell rang, which prompted the students outside for dismissal to the school buses. As we were on the bus, the driver threatened to turn the bus around and return to the school if the students did not take their seats. Papers were flying and things were thrown toward the front of the bus, striking the driver upside the head. "Who is the person that struck me in the back of the head with a pencil?" asked the bus driver. The driver became furious as he had his list of suspects. Brooke and her friends started it and I felt that I could not tell on my kid sister. I would talk to her when we got home and off the bus. As the bus approached our front yard, we stood up with our book bags on while slowly walking off the bus. I approached my sister to call her out on her wrongdoing and I then realized that our mother was standing at the front door waiting to greet us. Should I mention this to our mother or handle it myself?

CHAPTER 3

I was about to bring up what happened on the bus to my sister and then my mother started walking toward us as we got off the bus. "Mother, how was your day!" She could tell that I was nervous so she asked if everything was alright. That was all I could think of to say. I don't know why I give myself away like that, when I'm trying to hide something from my mother.

I could have told on my sister but deep down inside I didn't want to get her in trouble. She would never forgive me for bringing this up in front of our mother. At the same time, I knew that I couldn't allow her to get away with it without saying anything. I would approach her if I got the opportunity to speak with her alone. Brooke went into the house to start on her homework because she believed in getting good grades and participating in class. Besides, she had to keep her GPA up in order to stay on the basketball and baseball teams. It was time for me to slip off to my secret place so that I could pray. This was something that I'd always done. I had some type of special relationship with the Lord, however, I couldn't put my finger on it at the time. I truly agree with the saying that he's an on-time God! I noticed that if I prayed for anything in particular, the results were always quick and accurate. I really couldn't explain it, but I'd take the blessings over the curses any day. If anyone ever asked the question or wanted to know where my Bible was, my answer would be that it was with me. I had the pocket-sized New Testament version. It was given to me by an old lady that once gave me some great advice. She looked me in the eyes and said, "Son, you need to read your Bible because one day it'll be taken from you." At the time I didn't understand what she meant; however, she had a serious look in her eyes. She meant different versions of the Bible are always coming out; therefore, you need to have the word memorized and in your heart. I have learned that one word could change the whole meaning of a sentence in the Bible. She was murdered five years later by two individuals and this caused me to hold on to my Bible. I felt that the Lord put this Bible in my life for a greater reason, which was a lot to process at the time. As I was heading back to the house, I saw my sister outside with my mother.

"Eric, where have you been? You have missed dinner and I sent your sister out looking for you."

"I was off in the woods, Mother; I apologize if you guys were looking for me."

"Son, you are always disappearing into those woods. Why do you run off into the woods every day and disappear like that?"

"Sometimes, I just like to be to myself, Mother." She looked at me with disappointment.

"Eric, please go in there and warm your food up, son, before your sister throws it away right before she washes the dishes. I think it's actually your turn to wash the dishes and clean the dining area," Mom said.

Our mother made sure we took care of the chores around the house. I really should have been focusing on my math class because it was my weakest subject and it had been a struggle ever since the start of the class. It was even hard to stay focused on doing school work while my favorite TV shows were coming on. My mother threatened to cut the cable off if I failed my math class because she knows how much a good education means. Ethen was good at math, in case I had any questions. He was always willing to help his friend out; that's why he was my best friend. I would go over to his house but his parents were always arguing. They seemed to have a lot of marital problems. Sometimes I wondered how he was able to make straight As with all of that going on. I decided that I was going to call for him to come over and hang out. My phone was on the charger, which was half charged. I had a galaxy s9 and I loved the features on the phone. I really didn't care for the iPhone at all, so I had to go with the Samsung. As I reached down to pick the phone up, guess who was calling? It was Ethen doing his routine check on me to see how my math class was going. I cleared my throat to answer the phone.

"Hello, Ethen, how is it going bro?" He answered with an agitated voice.

"Nothing much, Eric, I was going to ask if I can come over. My parents are at it again and I need a quiet place to do some work," said Ethen.

"Come on over, buddy, I need some help with my math homework anyways," I said.

"Sure thing, Eric, I will be over in a few!"

Chapter 4

"Hello Ethen!" said my mom. "Come on in, the door is open. How are you doing?"

"I'm doing well. How are things going for you, Mrs. Jenny?" replied Ethen.

"I am doing well," she answered. "You don't have to call me Mrs. Jenny; call me Jenny. I know that you were taught how to properly greet people but all that is out of the door when you set foot in this house." Mom looked at Ethen as one of her children. "Eric happens to be in his room playing on that computer," said Mom. "I swear, that kid is going to turn into a program if he keeps it up." As she made her comment about her son she chuckled a bit.

Ethen walked down the hallway to my room and knocked. I answered the door with a smile on my face. "Hey Eric, did you ever finish that assignment for your math class?"

"No, I was waiting on you since you're the math expert. This stuff is really starting to get to me. I get so frustrated when it doesn't come easy."

"Well, Eric, you must be patient and let the problems come to you. You need to remember that each step is part of a process. You shouldn't look at or focus on the big picture; you must focus on each step of the problem. Let's look at your assignment for class," said Ethen."

They both reviewed the assignment and completed each problem. “Ethen, do you remember my cousin Jeremiah?”

“Yes,” replied Ethen. “I think he was in a gang or something like that. I remember your cousin from always getting into trouble. How is he doing?”

“Remember he went to jail at an early age for stealing cars and joyriding?” I asked.

“Eric, I just don’t understand your cousin,” said Ethen.” He always stayed in trouble with the law.” Maybe he has changed for the better, only time will tell.

“He is coming home this Sunday and I really hope that he gets his life together. While in the system he has gained the nickname ‘Bad News.’”

“I really don’t understand the name but I think it is an interesting name,” replied Ethen.

We talked until it was near bedtime and my mom stopped by the room to give a reminder that it was getting late.

"Boys, it's getting late and Ethen, you really should be heading home, dear," said my mom. Ethen gathered his things to leave.

Ethen really didn't think that his parents would notice that he had left the house. Shortly after Ethen left, I saw my mother making the rest of nightly rounds. She would talk to me for at least ten minutes before bedtime every night. We normally talked about the stories in the Bible and quoted verses to each other. The Bible had always been an interesting topic to me because I had always wanted to be connected with God. After she left my room, she requested that I say my prayers and get ready for bed.

CHAPTER 5

It was Wednesday morning as the school bell rung loudly in my ear. Mr. Fletcher was walking the halls and he was on a mission. He was passing out write-ups as if he was passing out awards. I couldn't wait until I was completely done with school. My mother always spoke of how important it was to have structure in your life, but structure was not my thing. I guess that's Mr. Fletcher's purpose; to teach us structure and responsibility.

I was on my way to my math class. Wednesdays

were always great because it was halfway through the week. All I could think about was the fact that my cousin was coming home and I had not seem him in a while. Mrs. Annie greeted me at the door as I entered the math class. I felt better and more prepared, thanks to Ethen. That was my pal; he had really helped me out with those assignments. Guess who got called to answer the first question of the today? Me that's who, and I was ready. I was so grateful because I really did not understand how I got some of my answers in earlier chapters. I always told myself on Fridays that I had the weekend to learn the whole book, which was never the case. That was just something that I told myself to feel better about my struggles in this subject area.

As the bell sounded for break time, I jumped up out of my seat to head to break. Ethen met me at my locker to ask how did I do on my assignment and performance in class. He was interested in how this class was going because he knew of all the problems that I have had in the past. We talked as we approached the vending machines.

"Eric, what are you getting for a snack today?" asked Ethen. "I would like some chips and a honey bun.

"Why did you ask, old friend?"

"I left my money at home by accident and I was trying to see if you had extra today," said Ethen. "Well, do you?"

"I have enough money to help you with purchasing a honey bun or chips, but not both."

"That is fine, Eric; I will take a honey bun. Thanks for your assistance," he made his response with sarcasm.

"You are welcome, Ethen! Have you seen Brooke? I need to make sure that she has what she needs. My poor sister is always forgetting her money at home." Then I saw her. "Hey Brooke, do you need anything today?"

"I am good Eric, thanks for checking," replied Brooke. "I did forget my money at home today; however, I borrowed money from a friend."

"That is not good; you really need to work on that. One of these days, you won't have anyone around to bail you out and you are going to be here starving."

"I will pray about that Eric, OK? You are always getting on my case. I know that you love me and you mean good. Please allow me to make my mistakes and learn from them." That's fine with me if she would like to learn life lessons.

"OK Brooke, I will allow you to do just that. It is almost the end of the week and I am so excited about seeing Jeremiah! Sunday can't come fast enough."

As we finished our last class of the day the bell sounded. I really did not have much to say on the bus ride home. As I was getting off the bus I saw someone hugging my mother from distance. When he turned around to look in my direction, I noticed that it was Bad News aka Jeremiah.

CHAPTER 6

"Look, Brooke, it's Jeremiah!"

"Eric, calm down," said Brooke. "You act like Jeremiah is someone special." She said this while walking off.

"Hello," said Jeremiah. I thought he was coming home Sunday but he was released early due to overcrowding.

"What was it like being locked up and away from home?" I asked.

"It was very difficult, Eric; it is a place that I am not trying to go back to." This was not the response that I was expecting. “I am trying to clean up my act and get my life together,” said Jeremiah. “I had to fight each and everyday in jail. We didn’t have access to go to the bathroom on our own and also had a poor choice of food daily. That is no place for me and I mean that.”

“Well it is good to see you out and free, cousin. You know that I look up to you, you’re like my role model.”

“That is good to know, Eric. You should know that I do not claim any gangs nor do I participate in any gang activities. I am trying to be a better person and make something of myself. Hey Eric, would you like to walk to the store with me?”

“Sure thing, let me tell my mother that we are going to the store.”

“Cool, I will be outside waiting.”

After speaking with my mother, we were on our way. "Mom said that it was cool; however, she asked for us not to walk down Martin Luther King Street due to the murder that took place out there last week," I told Jeremiah.

As we were walking we ran across a group of guys that were rivals of Jeremiah's old gang and he was recognized by one of the members. One guy said out loud, "Dude you have some nerves to walk past us and think that we are going to allow it to happen peacefully."

Jeremiah looked at the guy and said, "We don't want any problems."

The gang member answered Jeremiah by saying, "Well, you got a problem." He refused to allow us to walk past him and said over his dead body. My cousin then continued to walk forward and another guy charged him and the rest joined. Before I could join in to assist Jeremiah, he held his hands up and these guys fell to their knees begging for mercy. I didn't understand what I'd just witnessed. It was strange and I couldn't make sense of it. I could tell that this wasn't the first time that something like this had happened. It was almost like the gang of guys couldn't harm him and they fell to their knees while losing control of their bodies. Jeremiah saw the confused look on my face but he didn't make a comment about the incident. We then continued to walk to the store as though nothing had happened. I was too confused and stunned to ask any questions anyway.

When we got to the store, I saw Ethen. He was checking out at the register with his father. I walked up to him and spoke.

"Hello, Ethen, how are you doing old pal?"

"I'm doing well, Eric; just out shopping with my father. He wanted to come to the store to pick up a few things so I decided to ride along. I am so ready to go; we have been in this store for hours talking to people that he hasn't seen in years." That event that took place a few minutes ago was still on my mind.

I wanted to tell Ethen about the experience of what I had just witnessed with my cousin. I thought to myself that it would be better to save the story for another day. On our way home, Jeremiah talked about his experiences in jail. He didn't mention the incident that occurred on our way to the store. It would be a lie if I said that I wasn't curious about the incident that had took place.

CHAPTER 7

As we approached the house, I noticed that I was very tired. My eyes were trying to close on me constantly. Jeremiah looked at me and said, "Eric, you really should get some rest." I hope that Jeremiah didn't have anything to do with the way that I was feeling.

I wondered to myself if he was the cause of this sudden tiredness after what had happened on the way to the store. As I was walking down the hall to my bedroom my mother stopped me to check on me. She said that I looked as if I wasn't feeling well.

I mentioned to her that I was tired and wanted to lie down to take a nap. My bed felt so good and relaxing that I started drifting off. As I went into a deep sleep, I realized that I was starting to dream. In this dream I saw a young man playing baseball and everyone was cheering him on. The pitcher spit at the plate and then put his hands behind his back while looking at the young man. The pitcher threw the ball forward and this young man struck the ball, knocking it out of the universe. The people were cheering him on as if they were not surprise by him hitting the ball out of the universe. This dream really didn't make sense to me at all. What was the significance of someone hitting a ball out of the universe? I also had another dream that night that included me and a group of people being held hostage on a bus. I did not recognize any faces that were around me. In this dream, the guy did not have a face. When I asked him for his name, that was the moment that I woke up. It was like three in the morning and I then realized that I had been asleep for too long. I stayed up the rest of the night thinking about the dream because it seemed so real. I also turned on my game system to play NBA 2K until it was time to get ready for school. I actually fell asleep with the controller in my hand and my mother saw the light from the television in my room. She came in and asked me to get ready for school and she also asked me why was I so tired this morning. "Mom, I just had a long day yesterday, and besides that math class had me stressed out," I said.

My mother was always concerned about what we had going on in our lives, therefore, it was not uncommon for her to ask these questions. As I got out of the shower the bus was passing by the house. My sister was dressed and waiting on me. Our mother gave us a ride to school and on our way I was still thinking about the dream that I'd had the night before. I had these thoughts while approaching the school.

"OK guys we are here. Can y'all try to have a nice day at school and learn something?" Our mom asked.

"All right, Mom," I said. As we were walking into the front door of the school, we were approached by Mr. Fletcher.

"Why aren't you kids in class?" he asked.

"Mr. Fletcher, we are just now getting to school." Fletcher wanted to know where our parents were, and after learning that our mother had left the premises he issued us pink slips. Mr. Fletcher had been reminding all students that school was about to soon get out for the summer break and that they should avoid pink slips if possible.

At the end of the day, it was announced over the intercom that all final grades could be picked up after school hours at the office by parents, and we all prepared to board the buses to go home. Usually there were student fights at the end of the school year. Students would fight other students that they didn't like. This problem happened every year.

As we were getting on the bus to go home, I noticed that some of the students were arguing. I was expecting a fight on the bus because this was the end result every year. As we were on our way home, one student got up and walked up to another student and slapped him in the face. The student who was slapped was named Jimmy; he pulled a gun out. As he pulled the gun, he demanded that the bus driver keep driving. Jimmy aimed the loaded gun at the young man who had struck him in the face. Jimmy had a lot of rage in his face as he turned violent. He said that if anyone tried to call the police or tried anything stupid then he would start shooting.

CHAPTER 8

The driver did as he was told, but Jimmy didn't know that the driver had his phone right beside him. Cell phones were banned from school grounds, so Jimmy didn't think to check for phones. The driver had emergency assistance set up on his phone. He touched one button twice on the side of his phone and it sent out a notification of his whereabouts. His wife then notified the police and attempted to contact him by text message. Mr. Carter saw the message from his wife but chose not to respond due to the circumstance.

He didn't want to take a chance on blowing his advantage of having his phone. His attention immediately went to Jimmy and that gun that he had in his possession.

"I don't want to hurt anyone, but I will!" said Jimmy.

The police appeared to be riding behind the bus and asked the driver to pull over. Jimmy knew then that someone had to tip the police off so he demanded that all phones be thrown out the window of the moving bus. I just wanted to make sure that my younger sister was OK so I asked the gunman if she could sit with me and Jimmy's response was no.

"I am about to shoot the bully that slapped me in my face," said Jimmy.

Jimmy came to school every day and did his

work without any bad behaviors. He was bullied often by certain students because of the clothes that he wore and because he spoke differently, with an accent. The bus driver spoke up while trying to talk Jimmy into surrendering himself to the police. Jimmy had this look of rage in his eyes that could not be explained. It was almost like he had snapped because of the things that he had been through.

The bus was starting to run low on gas after hours of riding around in circles. Mr. Carter informed Jimmy of the low gas and told him that the bus would soon give out of gas. When the bus came to a complete stop, Jimmy felt that he had his back against the wall. There was no way out and he was trapped with a bus full of hostages. There were a long line of concerned parents and families waiting outside of the bus. Jimmy thought to himself that it was near the end and that he would spend a long time in prison for his actions. He felt that he had nothing to lose so he pointed the gun at his target; as he fired the shot the bus driver grabbed him from behind. This cause the bullet to fly in my direction, striking me in the chest. I fell backward while in the standing position.

The police and swat team charged the bus and took the perpetrator. The ambulance was called and medical attention was soon on site. I was carried to the nearest hospital and treated for a life-threatening gunshot wound. I was unconscious as my family waited on an update on my condition. The ER doctor spoke to my mother and told her that it was not looking good because the bullet had hit a main artery. While unconscious, I had an out-of-body experience. I appeared to be floating into another galaxy built somewhat like Earth; however, it was a world full of bad storms. It rained hard as I landed on the surface. I saw an area where houses used to be, but they were torn up by the storms. There were storm shelters everywhere, which was an obvious sign of life. I ran to the nearest shelter, as a tornado was forming within a half a mile away. The door was closed but unlocked and I climbed in and shut the door. I was looking around for people but did not see anyone.

Chapter 9

"Is anyone here?" I called out.

I did not receive an answer. I felt rumbling at the top of the shelter from the violent winds of the tornado that was passing by.

"Is this hell?" I wondered to myself. "Have I had an out-of-body experience at the hospital and been sent to witness this place?"

My next thought was to find someone to comfort me during these deadly storms. I was very concerned about the weather as I prayed for my safety. While I was praying for my safety, I could hear my mother's voice saying that God didn't create fear. The storms were violent and scary. I forced myself to have positive thoughts as I prepared to get through the hard time.

As the tornado passed by I reached to open the door to the storm shelter and I saw a man running. He was running for his life, screaming as he chased the tornado. It was almost like he wanted to commit suicide. I did not see anyone else as I looked around the other shelters in the area. I opened the door and saw another tornado on its way toward me. As the door shook harder this time it flew open and the winds of the storm lifted me and I flew up with the twister. I was flying, though it seemed as if I was standing still.

I heard a voice say, "You must witness and survive the storms of life in order to witness the individual gifts of the storm. There are three individuals total who have these gifts and powers. You must find each other and come together to face the storms."

I heard another familiar voice calling my name and it was my mother. "Eric, I love you so much and pray that you will pull through this." My eyes started moving and tried to open slowly.

I opened my eyes and told my mother that I loved her also. I realized that I did not have any pains in my chest nor did I feel any pain period. I asked my mother if we could go home and she said that I had been shot.

"Son, are you in pain?" she asked me. "I mean, baby, the doctors were telling me that you had a fifty-fifty chance of survival."

The doctor walked into the room and was in

shock to see me sitting up in the bed and asking to go home. He said that tests would need to be completed in order for me to be cleared to go home. As the tests came back, it seemed I was 100 percent healed. The doctors could not explain what had happened and said that it was a miracle.

While waiting on the decision to go home, I turned to the news and saw that Jimmy made the top story headlines. My mother then turned the television off and said that we didn't need a reminder of what had happened.

"I am just thankful that you are alive, baby," she said.

"I am happy also, Mom; this could have been a lot worse."

The doctor walked into the room and said

there was no reason for me to stay at the hospital; the test results were perfect. As we were walking out of the hospital, I saw Jeremiah. He didn't look surprised to see me up and walking around. I had questions for him because I didn't understand any of this. I then asked my mother if it would be OK for me to ride home with Jeremiah. While walking up to him, this feeling came over me that he was not who he appeared to be.

He looked at me and said, "Eric, you are all healed up now, so are you ready to talk? For you to heal so quick, you must have gone through the storm."

Chapter 10

"Yes, Jeremiah! How did you know this?"

"I had my experience while I was locked up," he said as we got into the car and began driving. "I got into a fight with another inmate and he stabbed me five times in the stomach. They rushed me to the nursing station; however, my injuries were fatal. I came back to life before they had a chance to contact the family. While going through the experience, I entered into this world just like ours; however, there were many storms going on at the same time. I was scared and felt alone. I ran into one of the storm shelters. The next thing that I remember is getting sucked out of the safe area. I was flying high in the sky and everything was still. I heard a voice speak, 'You must witness and survive the storms of life in order to witness the individual gifts of the storm. There are three individuals who have these gifts and powers. You must find each other and come together.' Eric, do you know your gifts or powers?" This was a question that I'm unsure of.

"I had a dream of the school bus hostage situation before it took place. I just thought that it was a déjà vu."

"You would not get your powers until after the storm. I had a dream also before my event took place. I am really not sure what to call that, Eric. You must discover your gifts as I have discovered mine," said Jeremiah. "I have the ability to control people's actions and speak to their minds. I heard your thoughts and that is how I knew about the experience."

"Jeremiah, so allow me to ask you this. Did you see anyone while in the storm shelter?"

"No, I did not see anyone nor did I hear anything other than the hail falling to the ground." The doors to the shelters have an inch of see through glass in the door. That's just enough sight to see which type of storm you're dealing with.

"Well, Jeremiah, I saw a man running, chasing a tornado while I was in the storm shelter."

"That must have been the third person," stated Jeremiah. "Only three individuals are allowed per lifetime. Eric, you are not allowed to mention this to anyone, and that includes your best friend. You would be punished by the storm if you mentioned this to anyone. If this information is mentioned to anyone that is not chosen, then that person would be cursed and would perish in the next natural disaster. You can only discuss this with the three chosen individuals. That is why I did not mention this to you until I was sure that you were one of the chosen ones. We must work together to find the third person who holds this power." We had an interesting conversation as we approached my neighborhood.

The car pulled up to the house as my mom came outside with a happy expression on her face. She was so happy that I was given a second chance at life.

"Eric, I will talk to you more tomorrow—and remember not to mention this to anyone said Jeremiah."

"OK, I gotcha!" I got out the car and ran up to my little sister and gave her the biggest hug ever. I thought that I would never see her again. Ethen came over to visit me and to welcome me home. I told him that I really didn't care to discuss the incident. He looked as if he understood. The real reason was that I was tempted to tell him about everything but I knew that it was not in my best interest. Lord knows that I would hate to lose my life in the next natural disaster. My mother prepared dinner and it smelled great. I asked if it was OK for Ethen to stay over and to have dinner with us. She did not have a problem with Ethen or anyone else staying over for dinner. She was just happy that I was alive. It's a blessing to get a second chance at anything, especially life; I was so thankful to be alive. There was a knock at the door. When I answered the door, it was Ethen's father. "Hello, Eric, how are you?"

"I am doing well, how about yourself?"

He reached to shake my hand, and as our hands touched I felt a serious sickness come all over me. I could feel the cancer that had already spread throughout his whole body.

CHAPTER 11

How will I tell my best friend that his father has cancer? What will I say? These were the thoughts that were running through my head. I wondered if his father knew of his condition and hadn't told anyone. It was possible this might be the reason he fought with his wife so much. I wondered if she knew that her husband had cancer.

It was really not my business to spread this information; however, Ethen was my best friend. A thought came to mind as I wondered all of these questions. I needed to speak with Ethen's father in private again. I would ask him some questions to see if he knew. Ethen stepped outside to have a personal conversation with his father. The suspense was killing me! As Ethen walked back into the house after his father left, I started asking personal questions about their medical history. Ethen mentioned that he had injured his hand by shutting it in door of his father's truck one day last week. This was the perfect opportunity to ask questions about their doctor and emergency visits.

"So Ethen, who is your family doctor?"

"What do you mean?" asked Ethen?

"I was just curious who was your family doctor. I remember that you mentioned that you jammed your finger in the door of your father's truck. Were you able to get that looked at?"

"No," replied Ethen. "Doctor Wilcox is his name, even though we haven't been in a while."

"When was the last time that your father went on a doctor's visit?"

"I'm not sure, Eric. You are starting to freak me out." That wasn't my intention at all, I was trying to gather information.

From the information that I gathered, I was able to determine that Ethen didn't know of his father's condition. Again I wondered, how do I tell my best friend that his father is dying? As Ethen glanced at his watch, he noticed that it was now 9:30 p.m. My mom walked in the room; she reminded us how late it was getting. Ethen knew what that meant.

"OK guys, I am about to head home," said Ethen.

I asked Ethen to find out more information on his father's visits with Dr. Wilcox. Ethen went home and asked his father some questions, which made him curious. He called me over the phone to get answers. The phone rung and I answered.

"Hello, Eric, this is Ethen's father."

"Hello!"

"I was calling because Ethen mentioned that you were inquiring about my medical history. Just what is it that you would like to know about my medical history?"

"I was asking Ethen about the last time you guys have been to the doctor and also who is your physician."

"Well, Eric, our physician is Dr. Wilcox. It has been about three weeks since I have been to the doctor's office," said Ethen's father. "Well, did you have any problems or sickness?"

"What do you mean, Eric?"

"Were you diagnosed with anything?"

Ethen's father paused in the middle of the conversation as he wondered where these questions were coming from.

"I have a question for you, Eric: how did you know?"

"Know what?"

"Actually, I was diagnosed with cancer on my last visit," said Ethen's father." "Please don't tell Ethen; I am not sure if he can handle this kind of information right now."

"Have you told your wife?"

"I have not told her yet; I guess that is why we have so many fights, because it frustrates me. The other day she asked for a divorce and since then I've had suicidal thoughts."

"Well, Eric, is it past your bedtime?" asked Ethen's father "We can finish talking about this situation later."

"OK, thanks for giving me this information and I promise not to mention this to Ethen."

"Thank you so much, and good night," said Ethen's father. The next morning came as the birds were chirping. I loved the sound of the birds in the early morning; it was the start of a beautiful day for me. I could smell the food and hot coffee boiling in the kitchen. "Good morning, Eric; where is your sister?" asked Mom.

"She's still in bed; you know how she likes to sleep late when school is out."

"Well she needs to get up before her food gets

cold," mom said. "I will wake her up after I eat," I replied.

"OK son!"

As I looked up Brooke was walking into the dining area.

"What is for breakfast, big bro?"

"Pancakes, sausage, and eggs," I replied.

Pancakes and eggs are Brooke's favorite breakfast foods. I started thinking about the conversation that I'd had with Ethen's father the night before. How would I be able to keep this information from my best friend and his mother? The great storms that I had witnessed were all supernatural and gave me such powers to see these things. It really hurt my feelings to receive information like this, especially when it was about a close friend's father. I still hadn't processed the fact that I was able to detect cancer within his body by skin-to-skin contact. Any other powers that I might have would also come to light as time passed. Having this gift made me feel as if I was living a dream.

As I was contemplating to myself, I saw a shadow from behind the wall. I knew this shadow and build from anywhere, but before I could say anything someone spoke.

"Hello, Eric."

It was Jeremiah!

CHAPTER 12

"I wanted to discuss with you in more detail about the third person in the storm," said Jeremiah. "This person has to be someone that escaped or will escape death." This person must have some type of supernatural ability and could possibly be searching for others with similar experiences.

"How do we find each other? Will this person approach us or would we approach him?" There were many questions about this mystery person, and the answers were not clear at the time. We will get this figured out and find our purpose.

There was a knock at the front door and it was Ethen. He wanted to know how the conversation with his father went the night before. He figured that his father would open up to me once we started conversing. I told him that I would have to talk to him later about it; I was in the middle of a conversation with my cousin. Ethen agreed to wait around because the suspense was bothering him. He felt that I knew something that he didn't know about his father. I asked Ethen to excuse us as we continued our conversation. Ethen excused himself from the area.

As Jeremiah and I spoke in private, Ethen was seated in the living room scrolling through the channels on the television. The television stopped on channel three, the local news station. The report spoke of a shooting that had occurred at the local mall, which resulted in three dead and one in critical condition. As all three of us approached the television to learn more information, Jeremiah and I glanced at each other as if we were thinking the same thing. I didn't mention the shooting or victims at this point. Jeremiah looked as if he had something to say.

"He could possibly be the third!" Jeremiah said out loud.

Ethen looked over at me and said, "What does he mean by that?"

I cleared it up by saying that this incident had been the third homicide investigation in the last couple of months. Ethen then gave me a funny look, which led me to think that he did not believe me. Jeremiah asked to see me in private once again. It was obvious that we were on the same page. We discussed how this person that was in critical condition could be the third survivor of the great storm. We decided to go to the hospital to get more information on this mystery guy and his condition. We left in a hurry to get to the hospital.

As we approached the front desk at the hospital, I saw a sign that said only family members were allowed in the ICU area for visits. I knew at this point that we would have to sneak in; that was the only way to visit this mystery guy. Jeremiah recognized one of the security guys and said that he was in good with him. He was a former guard at the institution where he had been locked up. There were two guards at the door; one guard asked for a visitor's pass. Jeremiah raised his right hand up and the guard went into a trance while losing control of his body. He knew the other guard and started a conversation with him. "Hello Mac!" said Jeremiah. Mac the guard looked surprised to see Jeremiah.

"What's up, Bad News?" replied the guard.

Jeremiah asked about the guy that was in critical condition and the guard informed him that he had passed way about two hours ago. He explained that the news reporters hadn't received that information yet. Jeremiah thanked him for the updated information and his time. This information was sad news and I felt for this young man's family. "Well, Eric, at least we know that he is not our guy," said Jeremiah.

As we were riding in the car, my mind started to wander off in different directions. I reminded myself that it comes a time when we must go back to the basics. I thought about the dream that I'd had the night before I got shot on the bus. I remembered seeing someone hitting a baseball out of the universe. Maybe this person had the power of strength, among other things. All of these were thoughts that were running through my head as we were on our way back to my house. We were determined to find this mystery person so that we could combine our powers. My first thought was the guy playing baseball.

Maybe I should consider joining the school's baseball team; that would be a great idea. This mystery person could be someone that had chosen not to show themselves. As we parked in the driveway, Jeremiah yelled my name to get my attention because I was daydreaming. There was a strange-looking man in the yard talking to my mother.

When I stepped out of the car, he looked at me and smiled. I stopped in silence and stared at him a bit.

He walked up to me and said, "Eric!"

I answered him and asked, "Sir, how do you know my name?" He looked at me and smiled again.

"I am a friend of your mother's," he replied.

He stated that he knew about the great storm but was not one of the chosen ones. I asked him to make sense of what he was saying because I was confused. He sat down and said that he had a brief story about how things work. I asked him how he knew of the great storm. He said that his brother was once a chosen one; however, he died from speaking about the secret. He stated that he was the person that his brother mentioned this information to. He felt that he contributed to his brother's death and blamed himself. He paused while giving me a blank stare.

“I have one question for you, why are you giving me all this information, I asked.

The old man responded by saying that he’d heard about the incident at the hospital and my miracle healing. He stated that it was obvious that I was affiliated with the great storm. I could not deny this information because it was public. The old man started explaining the process of the storm and how it works. The secret of the storm was to curse a person by killing them if they ever spoke on it with someone other than a survivor. When people die, they must first go through the storm before they can cross over to the other side. Everyone goes through the storm while facing life-threatening injuries, but most perish. There can only be three survivors living at a time and these three were the chosen ones. "Young man, I know of this information not because you've told but by experience. You don't have anything to worry about as long as you don't give me any information on the secret. I hope that you guys find each other, and good luck," said the old man.

CHAPTER 13

It was a lot to take in as I learned of all this new information. I heard the phone ringing in the living room so I asked my sister to bring it to me. I answered the phone and it was Ethen. He was in a panic!

"Eric, I do not know what to do."

"Ethen, calm down and tell me what is wrong, friend?"

"My father is being rushed to the hospital and the paramedics said that it is not looking good for him. My mother and I are on our way to the hospital, following behind the ambulance." I informed my mother that I was leaving before ending the phone call.

"OK, Ethen, I am on my way, friend." The phone call ended and I looked at my mother in disbelief.

I asked Jeremiah to give me a ride to the hospital and he was cool with it. As we walked up to the front counter, the clerk asked me to sign in. I told her that we were there waiting to see a friend of the family. By this time Ethen had called my cell phone and wanted to meet me in the area where his father was located. As we walked to the back and approached the room, I noticed that Ethen's father was out of the bed. This really did not make sense. I heard the toilet flush all of a sudden. He walked out and did not appear to be sick at all. He looked at us and asked Ethen if he was ready to go home.

Ethen had this look of confusion on his face. He reminded his father that his condition had worsened and that he had been near death. His father stated that he felt fine and assured us that nothing was wrong. The emergency room doctor walked in the room and asked everyone that was not immediate family to leave the room. Ethen's father said that it was fine if everyone stayed in the room while the doctor gave him the results.

The doctor looked at him and said, "For a dying man, your test results came back great." He was scratching his head while trying to figure out what had happened. The doctor explained that he would feel more comfortable if he ran more tests, just to be sure.

That's when I looked over at Jeremiah, and yes, we were thinking the same thing. I think that we had found our mystery guy, and it was Ethen's father. I did not like the idea of not mentioning this to Ethen, but I was happy that his father would be completely healed of all sickness. I began looking for the right time to approach him so that we could share information and combined our strengths.

"There was one question that does not make sense to me," I said. "What's that?" replied Jeremiah.

"The person hitting the ball out the universe was a kid, not a grown man. How could this be? Was I wrong in my dream?"

"Maybe your dream had some other significance other than what was obvious," Jeremiah replied.

Ethen's father overheard us talking and was interested in joining the conversation. "What are you guys talking about?" Now was the perfect time to get to know Ethen's father.

"So, Eric, how is it going?" he asked me.

"It is going well," I replied in a nervous voice.

All three of us were talking as we transitioned into the conversation of the great storm. We had to be careful not to give the information out too fast in case Ethan's father wasn't actually a survivor. I asked Ethen's father how was he able to heal up so fast after having cancer. He explained how he had a dream and in this dream there was a great storm. At the time, neither me nor Jeremiah gave out any signs that we were survivors of this storm. Ethen's father recalled seeing all types of storms and also spotting shelters along the ground. Most of them were damaged severely due to all of the storms. He saw these shelters and ran for cover and as he fell to the ground he was lifted by a tornado. He told the boys that he woke up immediately and mentioned this to his wife. Jeremiah and I looked at each other out of disbelief.

"You mentioned this to your wife?" I asked.

"Yes son, and it felt so real!" said Ethen's father. I was afraid for him after hearing this.

I ran to the television to find the nearest news station to see if any storms were forming. I was out of breath as I flipped the channels. Ethen's father wanted to know what caused this big panic but the boys did not want to mention it to him. The news did not mention any storms in the area nor the forecast for future storms. Ethen's father was in major trouble; however, we could not mention this to him. We were nervous and were ready to leave the hospital.

I told Ethen's father that we had to run and that we would check on him tomorrow. He wanted to thank us for coming by to see him in his time of need. On the way home Jeremiah and I had a conversation about the events that had taken place that day. It was obvious that Ethen's father had big problems. He really didn't know any better as far as how to handle the information about the storm. He didn't realize that he had put his life in danger by telling his wife of the secret.

"I wonder if he is safe in the hospital for the moment; they are releasing him tomorrow morning," I said. I wanted to tell Ethen so bad, but my life would be in danger. I thought that we had everything figured out until he delivered this information. Ethen's father was the third survivor; however, he gave out the secret information regarding the storm. I kept thinking about that dream I had the night before the shooting incident. It really didn't make sense, a kid hitting a ball out of the universe. As we pulled up to the driveway, I felt this feeling of fear. I immediately remembered what my mother always told me: God did not create fear. That made me feel better in a sense; however, it was easier said than done. Jeremiah glanced at me with his tired eyes.

"Goodnight, Eric!" said Jeremiah. "I will see you tomorrow; you really should get some rest." We both needed to get some rest; we'd had a long and unforgettable week.

CHAPTER 14

The next morning came and the birds were chirping. Brooke ran into my room screaming, "Eric, wake up! The news is on and one of my classmates was in a bad car wreck. They are saying that he has life-threatening injuries and was rushed to the emergency room." I felt bad for her classmate. She seemed to be fine so I asked her to keep me updated on his condition.

As I walked outside, I noticed that the clouds were getting dark, as if it was about to storm. My mother pulled up; she had just run to the store to get groceries. I ran to the car to help my mother bring the groceries in before it started raining. You could hear the thunder in the clouds as the storm approached. As I took my phone off the charger, I saw that I had seven missed calls. All seven calls were from Jeremiah. I called him back immediately and he told me that Ethen's father had been struck dead by lightning while being too close to the window at the hospital. This was terrible news and I had to get to the hospital as soon as possible. Brooke asked if she could ride to the hospital with us so that she could visit her classmate. We rode in complete silence while I was in deep thought. We pulled up to the hospital and I started to feel nervous.

As we were walking toward the help desk, the attendant was very nice and helpful. After she found out that we were there to visit and inquire about Ethen's father, she then mentioned the information regarding what had happened to him. The attendant said that Ethen's father was pacing back and forth, thinking about his marriage. He mentioned his wife and how much he loved her. He was talking about the problems that they were having and that he hoped that their marriage could be saved. Lightning came out the sky as if he was the intended target of the strike.

"It was crazy and the most scary thing that I've ever experienced," said the attendant." "Are you guys related to him?"

"No, he is my best friend's father," I said.

Brooke walked in the room and said that her friend was in critical condition and that he could only have visits from close family. Brooke mentioned that he was good in baseball; he was known as a great home-run threat. Jeremiah looked at me as if everything was starting to come together. We asked Brooke for some privacy to converse about this new information. Brooke left the room as requested.

"Eric, I think that this is our guy!" said Jeremiah. "We must first wait to see if he survives the storm." As Jeremiah talked something told me to check my phone.

I looked at my cell phone and realized that my mother had called. I called her back and she wanted to know how Brooke's friend was doing. I gave her the update on Brooke's friend and also told her about Ethen's father. She was in shock about the information about Ethen's father. She mentioned that he was such a good person and he always seemed to be happy.

"I really hate that for him and his family," she said. "Eric, have you spoke with Ethen or called to check on him?"

"I saw him at the hospital yesterday and spoke with him and he was fine; however, I am sure that this will hurt him."

"All you can do is be there for him," said Mom. I agreed with my mother.

We ended the phone call and I continued my discussion about the great storm. The storm continued but the conditions were not as bad as before. My mother was concerned about us being out in this dangerous weather. The phone rang again and it was my mother calling to ask me to come home.

"Son, it is about time for you to come home and I am worried about you."

"Yes Mom, we will be home in a few. I was trying to get more information on what happened to Ethen's father."

"I understand, son, but I need for you and your sister to come home immediately."

Chapter 15

When we got home, my mother caught me as I was walking in the door and gave me the biggest hug. She whispered in my ear, "Everything will be OK, son, you just have to pray about these things." All I could do was agree with her but the truth of the situation hurt.

It was getting late as I looked at the time on my phone. I knew that I was going to have a long restless night after all that had happened that day. There was a knock at the door, and when Brooke answered it was Ethen. He had this dry, dull look on his face. I really didn't know what to say to him after just losing his father. I knew that he was devastated about the situation. All I could do was be here for my friend and try to comfort him during the grieving process. "Hey, Ethen, I am sorry to hear about your father. If you need me, you know that I am here for you with anything that you may need." "I know Eric, you are such a great friend." I wanted to check on his mother also.

"Where is your mother?"

"She was heading toward the hospital and now she is not answering her phone," said Ethen. Ethen said that he had not spoken with his mother since earlier in the day. "Eric, I think my mother has a boyfriend and has for sometime now."

"What do you mean, Ethen?"

"I didn't tell anyone; however, I came home

early from school one day and there was a man sitting on the couch in our home. My mother said that he was selling life insurance but this guy was not dressed up. I had a strong feeling that she was keeping information from me. I think that my father knew that she was having an affair."

"Why do you say that?" I asked. He told me that his father had asked her if she was having an affair. There was talk around town that she had a boyfriend.

"I don't mean to be telling my mother's business, but I feel that I can talk to you," said Ethen.

"You're right, best friend, you can tell me anything."

We talked until the next morning came. My mother walked into the room and spoke to Ethen. She gave her condolences to Ethen and asked if there was anything that she could do. My sister walked into the room and told us that her friend was better and was approved to have visitors. I got on the phone and called Jeremiah to ask for a ride to the hospital. He really wanted to meet this kid, so I reminded him to watch his speed on the highway. While we were waiting on Jeremiah to arrive, my mother asked what we had planned for the day. I told her that we were planning to go and visit Brooke's friend who was in that bad wreck. She was hoping to hear some good news about that young man and prayed that he had a speedy recovery. We were waiting on Jeremiah to pick us up.

Jeremiah pulled up and we got in the car and left, heading to the hospital. Brooke sat in the back seat and Ethen didn't want to tag along for emotional reasons. As we pulled up to the hospital, I felt that if I'd spent a lot of my time there recently. We approached the front desk and the lady recognized us. She asked who we had come to see this time. She asked if we were close friends of the patient, to which we said no. She responded by saying that she would let us go back there because of the incident that had happened the night before. As we walked into the room, I saw him sitting up in the bed. He looked at us and recognized my sister. They spoke to each other and he was wondering why all of us came in to see him. She called him by his name, which was Cory. I asked Brooke if she could give us a moment to speak with her friend. As she closed the door, I asked him how was he feeling.

"I feel pretty good; I didn't catch your name," said Cory.

"It's Eric, and this is my cousin Jeremiah."

I asked him about his recovery and how did he think he had healed so fast. He told me that he'd had a dream and had visited a place where there were many storms. He said that storm shelters were all around; however, he ran and got into a ditch. Cory didn't think that the shelters were safe; he had no idea of what was in them. He also said that he saw two people go into the storm shelters. Each went into separate shelters and he didn't know if there were more people. I then realized that he might have seen me in the shelter. He must have been the person that I saw running past me during the storm. How could all three of us witness the storm at the same time when our incidents took place at different times? I didn't know the answer to that question but it looked as if we had found our third survivor!

Chapter 16

There was a slight knock at the door and it was the doctor. He confirmed that Cory was in great condition to go home. He asked him to check out at the front desk on the way out. I couldn't wait for all three of us to get together to see what powers we had as one. Cory gave us his address and asked if he could have some time with his family before we met up.

On our way back home I wanted to stop by Wendy's to get a triple cheeseburger and fries. We made a quick stop as my sister ran inside to use the restroom. As I looked at passing cars in the parking lot, I happened to see Ethen's mother pulling up to the drive thru. She had a nice-looking young man with her. As they placed their order, he reached over and kissed her. I couldn't believe what I'd seen; Ethen's mother had her lover in the car with her. They looked so happy together, I was confused.

My sister comes out of Wendy's and got back in the car. "Is that Ethen's mother, Eric?" Brooke asked. Brooke felt sure of what she was asking me.

I ignored her and we got back on the road so I turned the music up to avoid any other questions. As we pulled up in my driveway, I received a text from Cory. He asked if we could meet now instead of later. He said something about having dinner plans later on with his parents and grandparents.

We dropped Brooke off at the house and put the address that Cory had given us into the GPS. He lived about twenty minutes away from my house. As we arrived, we noticed he lived in a gated community; you could tell that his folks had money. As I knocked on the door, I saw this pretty older lady come to the door. She looked at me and smiled while saying, "Cory will be out shortly." I waited shortly.

Cory came outside and the three of us got to talking. I asked him about his powers and special gifts. He said that he had super strength and power. He had an old baseball bat lying around in the yard. He picked it up to demonstrate his strength. I tossed him the ball and he knocked it out of the universe. I was amazed as to what I witnessed, even though I'd already seen it in a vision.

Chapter 17

It was getting close to Cory's dinner time with his family so we prepared to leave by walking toward the car. It was interesting meeting up with the third survivor of the storm. On the way home, it started to rain. I had left my umbrella at the house and Jeremiah didn't have one. The phone rang and it was Brooke; she wanted to know how Cory was doing.

"Hello, big bro, how is my friend Cory?" asked Brooke.

"He's doing well."

"Why did you guys go and visit him?" asked Brooke.

"Brooke, what is it to you?" I replied.

"I was just curious because you guys don't even know him."

"Hold on, Brooke, I have a beep from the other line."

It was Cory calling me back wanting to get more information on our next move. I told him that we would meet up the next day again. He was satisfied with that answer. I was extremely tired from all of the moving around we had done during the day. I was so happy to see my house; I got out of the car and told Jeremiah goodnight.

As I was walking down the hallway to my room, I saw my mother praying near her bed. I walked into my room and laid across the bed and fell asleep. The next morning came and I heard my mother calling my name.

"Eric, Jeremiah is on the phone."

He didn't normally call this early in the morning so I rushed to get to the phone.

"What's up, Jeremiah!"

"I'm good, what all do you have planned for today?" Jeremiah asked.

"Nothing much, cousin. I was going to ask Brooke if she wanted to have a movie night."

"Cory called asking to hang out with us today if possible," said Jeremiah.

"Did he give you a time?"

"He would like to meet up within the next hour or so."

My mother walked in and asked if I could cut the grass and trim the hedges around the house. I explained to her that I would as soon as I get back from visiting Cory. She didn't have a problem with that at all. Jeremiah wanted to leave a little early because he drives very slow to avoid accidents. Yes, he's that type of driver. As we pulled up in Cory's yard, he was walking out of the door.

"Hello guys!" said Cory. We spoke back to him and Cory got into the car. He wanted to go to this park about three miles in town and talk. While we were on our way, a big truck recklessly ran us off the road, causing the car to flip over ten times while landing in a body of water. All three of us had to be airlifted to the nearest hospital for our injuries. All three of us had life-threatening injuries. I felt my spirit leave my body and I began to float. I had done this before so I wondered if this was it for me. As I landed, I noticed that I was in the same place again where all the storms were happening. I saw two people hiding in a ditch and they were getting rained on. I yelled for help and they ran toward me. It was Cory and Jeremiah!

CHAPTER 18

We took cover together at a nearby shelter. The winds were now blowing at least 100 miles an hour. The storm was not slowing down and was very dangerous. Hail started falling and this was a sign of another tornado being close by. The door started shaking like it was about to fly open. All three of us pulled on the door with all of our might. We were looking through the built in glass that was made in the door. We saw a tree go flying by with the wind—this was a full-sized tree with the roots and all.

Once the tornado passed by, the ground started to shake heavily; it was an earthquake. It seemed as if it was one thing after another. I wondered what the mission and purpose was for all of this.

Cory was the first to speak: "I hope this is not a permanent visit." He was shaking his head while looking frightened.

As he spoke, we saw a man running for his life in the storm. I yelled to get his attention.

"Hey sir!" The guy ran toward us, scared for his life. I felt as if I'd seen this guy somewhere before; I don't forget a face. This guy was trying to figure out what was going on. He didn't understand anything that was happening. I asked him about any incidents that may have occurred as of recent. He mentioned that he had a girlfriend and a stepson that he would be leaving behind. He didn't have any pictures on him of his family at the time. We all were frustrated with all these storms and damaging winds that were happening back to back. Another earthquake started, which caused a tsunami with waves of water coming in our direction. Jeremiah yelled, "Run for cover!" We all ran for shelter and safety at the same time. We just did make it to safety and were very thankful to survive this disaster. I tried to open the door to the shelter but it was stuck from all of the water that was above us. Cory had the strength to break through; however, we could drown from all the water above us. It was best that we wait this storm out. We didn't have any food in this shelter and had no clue on when the water would clear.

"I didn't get your name," said Jeremiah.

"My name is Jerry; I forgot to mention my

name due to the circumstances. I apologize for that."

"It's OK," said Jeremiah. "This is my cousin Eric and our friend Cory. We are survivors of the first storms and are back for the second time somehow."

"This is my first time experiencing the storm," said Jerry. "I believe that I'm here because of how I've being living. I haven't been living right guys, I'll be the first to admit. I've been dishonest and taking money at my job. I'm an accountant by profession. I also have a confession to make about something that I've been wanting to get off my chest. I was dating this beautiful woman that was married. She didn't get alone with her husband. Her husband was later diagnosed with cancer. He was recently killed in a violent storm in the area where they lived. I met her at that superfoods while she was grocery shopping. I remember seeing her walking the aisles looking for cranberry juice. I followed her and then walked up to her to start a conversation. She mentioned that she was married and was off limits. I gave her my number and asked her to keep it even if she didn't call. "One day she called me after having an argument with her husband. We started off as friends and then things got interesting all of a sudden. We started dating about a year ago and I knew then that I wanted her to myself. She promised me that she was going to leave him but later found out that he had cancer.

"I know that what I'm doing isn't right, but I was in love with her. We'd go to bingo every Wednesday night and out to eat afterward. We share the same thoughts and get along great with each other. I would do anything to be with her. Everyone keeps telling me that I went about getting her the wrong way, but I really love her. I recently met her son for the first time and he's a great kid." Then he suddenly paused as if he was talking too much.

"What's her son's name?" asked Jeremiah.

"His name is Ethen," replied Jerry.

CHAPTER 19

I couldn't believe the information that I'd just received about this guy and Ethen's mother. As we closed the conversation the wind almost blew the door off on the shelter. Things went quiet for a moment. I think that everyone was getting a little nervous about this whole situation with the storm. We needed to come up with a plan to survive these storms, but if we decide to run, where would we run to? I thought that it would be best if we left the storm shelter and explored the area to help find our way up and out of there. Jeremiah came up with a plan to escape and to help with safety. He wanted to find a better shelter and wait the storm out. This wasn't a good plan in my opinion. Jerry had a concerned look on his face as if he wanted to get something off his chest. He mentioned a situation that happened during the storm previously.

"I met this guy and his name was Clifton," said Jerry. "He was the first person that I saw when I entered into the storm. Clifton didn't make it through the storm. We were running and he ran into a pothole, which caused him to get injured. He asked me to keep running for cover because he knew that he would be a burden. I tried to carry him with all of my might but the strong winds lifted us off the ground. We were then separated without a trace. He had been in the storm for quite some time and he mentioned that the only way out was to be chosen. He also mentioned that the storm could be defeated. In the moment of facing the storm, your faith could clear the weather and return everything back to normal. He mentioned that these storms were created by poor faith and poor faith alone. The storms have never been defeated by mankind. It has to be defeated by one of the chosen survivors. I was told that there are families in this area but they have taken cover due to the storms. The shelters won't be able to hold much longer due to the pressure of the winds and water. There are only two options—either perish or defeat the storm. There are many kids and families facing these storms. People are running out of food and water. These storms are very dangerous, therefore it's not in our best interest to split up at anytime."

CHAPTER 20

These powerful storms were coming back to back. The water was making it difficult to see on the outside of the shelter. We decided that we would have to open the door to get a better view.

As we opened the door to check out the weather that we were dealing with, the wind pushed the door open. The rain was falling hard and it took two people to shut the door. I ran across the street to see if we could find a better shelter because the one that we were in wouldn't last much longer. As

I ran, I saw a lady running with a baby in her arms. I yelled to get her attention and she looked back while losing her balance. I ran over to assist her with the baby. She pointed to a nearby shelter that her family was in. I picked up the baby and we went to their shelter.

As we opened the door I saw three kids and one appeared to be sick. He was wrapped up in bandages and lying on a table. The woman mentioned that her husband had been killed out in the storm while trying to get food for the family. I asked her how they got here and she said that they were all in a van on a family trip when an eighteen-wheeler hit them on the interstate. When they woke up, they were in this world of storms. She mentioned that they were running out of food and asked if I had any to spare. I ran back to the shelter with my family and friends to bring them over to this one. We gathered all the food and took it over to them so that we would all have enough to eat. I asked Jeremiah to make a run with me to find more food and materials that could be used. The wind speeds immediately picked up as a tornado was passing over the shelter. The winds were lifting the door and it took three of us to hold the door steady. We ran out into the storm to make a food run and the ground started shaking; we were in an earthquake. This was a big one and it broke the ground in half. Cory yelled, "You guys be careful out there!" Everyone survived the earthquake.

I really started thinking about defeating this storm. What's the purpose of surviving these storms every twenty minutes if it never ends?

CHAPTER 21

I heard thunder above as it rained even harder. Jeremiah spotted a vacant shelter and we went in to check it out. There was a bag of clothes on the floor near a shelf full of food. It was too much food to take in one trip back to our shelter. This happened to look like a nice place to hang out during the storms. I often wondered what happened to the people that didn't survive the storm. We were given certain powers and gifts from surviving the storm the first time, but these powers didn't work in this place. I feel helpless without the opportunity to use my gift. We were looking for answers on how to defeat this storm so that we could return back to our planet.

There was no warning on what type of storm was coming or taking place. I tried to open the door but it was too heavy and water started leaking in the cracks. It was possible that we were experiencing another tsunami. Jeremiah was afraid, but for some reason I wasn't afraid. I once again thought about my mother and her saying on how God did not create fear. After two days of waiting for the door to lighten, we were able to lift the door and get out. The dirt had turned to sand and it was clear to see that the area had flooded. We returned to the shelter where Cory and everyone was waiting on food. Cory had a concerned look on his face while asking about the food.

"Hey, Eric, is that all the food that you guys could come up with?" Cory asked.

"No, there is plenty more where that came from. We just have to go back and get it." He was concerned about food, while I was focused on getting out of this place.

I felt as if I was in charge and the leader of this group. We had to work together to get out of this world. I really missed my family and friends back home. I wanted for the group to come together and have a prayer session. I didn't feel fear; however, I was concerned about getting home. I walked over to the sick kid and he had a Bible lying on the table beside him. It looked as if someone was reading it and praying over him. I reached and got the Bible. As I opened it up, I felt this spirit come over me. I chose to flip the pages and start reading wherever the pages stopped. The page stopped on 2 Corinthians 12:9: "But he said to me, My grace is sufficient for you, for my power is made perfect in weakness. Therefore I will boast all the more gladly of my weaknesses, so that the power of Christ may rest upon me." This Bible verse gave me the strength and courage to face the storm.

"Eric, do you think that it'd be best for all three of the chosen one's to defeat the storm?" Jeremiah asked.

"That may be the best option," I replied. "I mean there are three chosen survivors; that might be our purpose. We were told that you must defeat the storm by faith and faith alone. We have many people that are about to run out of food soon, so we really need to make a move and take a chance."

"I'm with you guys," said Cory.

"Standing in front of the storm is like committing suicide," I said. "We first need to figure out what is possibly starting these storms and why it is consistent. It seems as if the storms are all coming from one direction. We should run in that direction until our destination is reached."

"Without our power and gifts we are weak against the storm," said Cory.

The other guys ignored Cory's response as they prepared to make a move. I had faith that we would reach our destination and figure out where these storms were coming from so that we could stop them. The winds were blowing so hard that we could hear the sounds of it. We had to move quickly before another deadly storm came in our path. Hail started to drop and there was a loud roar in the sky. We knew that meant a tornado was approaching, and the guys and I took cover until it passed. Jerry was concerned and said that he was tired of all these storms coming back to back. A tornado dropped out of the sky and it was moving fast. We ran for cover and this storm was right on us. As I opened the door to the storm shelter that was nearby, we saw it was very small in size. Jerry was last to enter and while he was trying to shut the door it flew open. Jerry started yelling for help, so I reached for him and missed his hands. He was lifted and carried out by the tornado. The room was full of sadness after this moment.

We waited for the storm to clear out before moving forward. We vowed to stick together during this journey. We left the storm shelter and made a run for it as the winds pushed against our bodies.

As we were passing a nearby shelter, I noticed that the door was open. I wanted to look inside to see what we could find. There were two dead bodies inside and one injured person. I approached this guy to check on him.

"Hello, sir, can you tell me your name?" He prepared to speak as he struggled to situate his legs.

"My name is Seth and I was hit by the debris from one of the tornadoes. There's a war going on with these storms and we're losing big time," said Seth. "Where are you guys headed?"

"We are headed to the main location where these storms are coming from."

"Well, good luck with that guys; I just fight to survive for myself," replied Seth. "Besides, my leg is injured too bad to run from any storm that crosses my path. I'm better off staying here and praying that you guys find a way to defeat the storm." I looked around and noticed a table full of food.

They had plenty of food so we sat around and ate before returning on our journey.

I heard some people talking while standing above the shelter and I didn't recognize any of the voices. We sat quietly because they could have possibly had bad intentions if we were discovered. Once they left the area, we continued on our journey. Another storm was approaching, because the clouds were very dark. Three tornadoes dropped out of the sky at one time. This was the worst we'd seen since visiting this place. We took off to run for cover and one of the twisters was too close to me. I turned around and decided to face the storms, because for one I didn't have a choice. I remembered what my mother always said: God didn't create fear. I stood as the tornadoes approached me. Cory and Jeremiah joined me to face the storms.

We were lifted up by the twisters and I heard a voice that said, "My grace is sufficient for you, for my power is made perfect in weakness. Therefore I will boast all the more gladly of my weaknesses, so that the power of Christ may rest upon me." I then remembered that faith and faith alone defeated the storm. We all had powers and special gifts that were created by going through the storm. We didn't need special powers to overcome these storms; we only needed faith.

At that moment, I heard the sound of my mother's voice and I opened my eyes. I noticed that I was lying in my bed as though nothing had happened. The phone rang and it was Jeremiah with Cory calling on three-way.

"Hey Eric, it looks like we defeated the storm!" said Jeremiah. "Yes, we did!"

"I got Cory on the line with us," said Jeremiah.

"Thanks for letting me know!"

"We called to thank you for saving our lives during the storms," said Jeremiah. "All of those people that were in the world of the storms were saved by our faith. I can honestly say that I'm proud to be one of the chosen ones. If you wouldn't have turned around to face the storm, then we wouldn't have survived. All Glory to God, he gets all the praises!"

SUMMARY

There are storms in our everyday lives. The storms in this story represent the storms of life. Some people survive and some are unfortunate. If you have God on your side and trust in His word then you can too survive any storm, including the greatest storm. The Lord will give you the right tools to make it through the storm; however, it is up to you to choose the right path. Eric, Jeremiah, and Cory all chose the right path and that's how they survived the storm. They used the tools and received powers and gifts for surviving the storms.

When you face the greatest storms of your life, how will you respond? Are you a survivor of the storm or will you fail to choose the right path? Ethen's father faced the Great Storm; however, he mentioned this to his wife and not to the people of the storm. He lost his life because only faith could have helped him get through these storms and not people of the world. Faith gave them the power over the storm!

CPSIA information can be obtained
at www.ICGtesting.com
Printed in the USA
BVHW071136040419
544607BV00001B/154/P

9 781977 208774